Maddy McGuire, CEO

Bring Back the Bees

Calico

An Imprint of Magic Wagon
abdopublishing.com

By Emma Bland Smith Illustrated by Lissy Marlin

For all my San Francisco neighbors and community, on
12th Avenue and beyond–EBS

To my lucky stars, thanks for lighting my way–LM

abdopublishing.com

Published by Magic Wagon, a division of ABDO, PO Box 398166,
Minneapolis, Minnesota 55439. Copyright © 2019 by Abdo
Consulting Group, Inc. International copyrights reserved in all
countries. No part of this book may be reproduced in any form
without written permission from the publisher. Calico™ is a
trademark and logo of Magic Wagon.

Printed in the United States of America, North Mankato,
Minnesota.
052018
092018

Written by Emma Bland Smith
Illustrated by Lissy Marlin
Edited by Bridget O'Brien
Art Directed by Laura Mitchell

Library of Congress Control Number: 2018931814

Publisher's Cataloging-in-Publication Data

Names: Smith, Emma Bland, author. | Marlin, Lissy, illustrator.
Title: Bring back the bees / by Emma Bland Smith; illustrated by Lissy Marlin.
Description: Minneapolis, Minnesota : Magic Wagon, 2019. | Series: Maddy
    McGuire, CEO
Summary: When Maddy learns that bees are fast becoming endangered, she wants
    to help by bringing a hive to her school. Unfortunately, the beekeeper at the
    community garden is struggling with her business. Maddy comes up with her
    sweetest plan yet: a honey-focused booth at the farmers market. The profits
    will save the beekeeper's business and the beekeeper will give Maddy's school
    its own hive. Maddy's learned a lot about business, but things get sticky when
    she translates her skills to the conservation world.
Identifiers: ISBN 9781532131837 (lib.bdg.) | ISBN 9781532132230 (ebook) |
    ISBN 9781532132438 (Read-to-me ebook)
Subjects: LCSH: Bees--Juvenile fiction. | Wildlife conservation--Juvenile fiction. |
    Farmers' markets--Juvenile fiction. | School gardens--Juvenile fiction.
Classification: DDC [E]--dc23

TABLE OF CONTENTS

Chapter One
For the Love of Guacamole 4

Chapter Two
The Pitch. 14

Chapter Three
Morning Meeting in the Garden. 26

Chapter Four
Visit to the Beehive 34

Chapter Five
A Sweet Plan 48

Chapter Six
A Business Proposition 58

Chapter Seven
Sponsored! 67

Chapter Eight
At the Farmers Market 77

Chapter Nine
Stickier and Stickier 88

Chapter Ten
The Simple Things. 98

Chapter One

Through the glass, Maddy watched a bee enter the hive. Another bee exited. At least she assumed it was a new one. They looked the same to her.

The bee paused on the ledge, then took flight. It flew out the science museum window and disappeared.

Probably to drink from some yummy flowers, thought Maddy. She stared intently, looking for more bee action.

"What are you waiting for, bees? There's lots of nectar out there!"

"Maddy!"

She jumped. "You scared me!" she said to her older brother, Drew.

Drew lifted a shoulder. "Sorry. What are you looking at?"

Maddy pointed. "Bees! Well, there were some before anyway. I don't see any more."

But Drew had moved on. "Mom says it's time to go. We're going to stop by the farmers market. Maybe we can get a cheese roll. Come on!"

He ran toward the front of the museum. A *T. rex* skeleton stood guard inside the huge glass doors. But Maddy turned back to the bees.

She walked over to a placard and read it. *Honey bees are diminishing in number across the United States, threatened by habitat destruction, pesticides, and monoculture.*

There were a lot of big words in that sentence. But Maddy got the idea. Bees were in danger.

She read on. *Why does this matter? Bees pollinate many of the crops that grow in our nation. If we lose bees, we lose our food source. What can we do about it?*

Maddy started to read on. But another hand on her shoulder pulled her back into the moment.

"Mads, time to go," said her mom. "The market closes at one."

Drew was already outside the museum. "I'm starving!" he called as Maddy and Mom approached. "I hardly ate anything today!"

"Um, do you call three waffles with chocolate sauce and a boatload of maple syrup nothing?" said Maddy. She followed him down the steps.

"Oh yeah, I forgot," he called back.

"Metabolism of a rabbit," said Mom, walking alongside Maddy. "I wish I was thirteen again."

Maddy wasn't exactly hungry. But her stomach felt hollow, in a way she couldn't exactly identify.

She couldn't stop thinking about the bees. But she did love cheese rolls. She hurried to catch up with Drew.

They walked through the park under cherry trees dripping with fluffy blooms. Yellow daffodils poked through the green grass. A robin pulled a worm from the earth. And a gopher pushed its head out of its hole.

Maddy loved spring. Everything felt fresh and new.

Finally, they reached the end of the park. That's where the farmers market set up every Sunday.

Mom pulled scrunched-up shopping bags and a list from her purse. Then she opened her wallet.

"Okay, guys, here's five dollars." She handed the bill to Drew. "That should be enough to buy two cheese rolls. Bring me the change, okay?"

"Thanks, Mom!" Drew grabbed the bill and sprinted past the produce stands. "Maddy, I'll get you one."

Mom strode off to shop for veggies, leaving Maddy to stroll on her own. Maddy waved to a few neighbors, but didn't feel like stopping to talk.

She paused at the Lopez Farm stand. They sold baby zucchini. Her mom sometimes fried it in olive oil.

At the Three Crows Ranch stand, she skirted a line ten people-long. They were waiting for strawberries. One basket cost five dollars. But most people thought they were worth it.

At Clover Valley's booth, a farmer stood holding a platter. It had slices of avocado on toothpicks, sprinkled with sea salt.

"Free sample?" the farmer asked.

Maddy took one, letting the buttery flesh melt in her mouth.

"Makes great guacamole!" the farmer added.

Maddy loved guacamole. Suddenly, she felt another pang in her stomach. Hunger, yes, but mixed with something else, too.

Panic. If bees disappeared, she realized, then would these yummy foods disappear, too? Including guacamole?

She turned back to the farmer. She'd better stock up. "Um, can I have ten avocados? Or maybe twenty? I'll be right back with money!" And she ran off to find her mom.

Chapter Two

Walking home, Drew chattered about his school's upcoming science fair. Maddy transferred the heavy bag of avocados from one hand to the other. She munched on her cheese roll. Mom lugged another bag of veggies.

"Will's going to do this thing where you put food coloring in water. And then you put a plant in it, and see if the plant changes color," he said.

Plants. That made Maddy think about bees.

"And Charlie's going to hatch butterflies."

Butterflies. Insects. That made Maddy think about bees, too.

"I was thinking of seeing how avocado reacts to different kinds of light."

Avocados! Ahhh! Maddy kicked the sidewalk. Why was everything reminding her of bees? And the fact that they might disappear forever. And maybe her favorite foods, too.

Maddy wished she could do something about it. But science wasn't really her strong point. At least it hadn't been so far.

Of course, Maddy used to think she was bad at math, too. But that changed when she was planning her last few businesses. She'd realized she was actually pretty good at it.

Maybe Maddy could do something to help the bees. But what?

She dropped the paper bag her cheese roll had come in into her family's green compost bin. It was next to their house. She walked slowly up the steps.

What had the placard said about the factors threatening bees? There had been a big word. *Monoculture.* What did that mean?

Maddy darted past Drew going through the front door. She dropped her bag, and ran to the laptop. She found it closed on the living room desk.

She grabbed it and plopped down on the living room couch. She opened a dictionary website.

Monoculture, she typed in. *The agricultural practice of planting one crop across large areas rather than a variety.*

Why was that bad for bees? she wondered. Next, she did a search for "bees" and "threats."

Maddy found a government website with an explanation. Small family farms were being bought up by large farms. The large farms tended to specialize in just one crop.

This caused several problems for bees. For example, all the crops bloom at once. When the bloom was over, the bees found themselves stuck with no nearby flowers to visit.

Maddy skimmed the article. And then her eyes widened. *People can help by installing hives in cities, where bees have access to the large diversity of urban plants.*

She slammed the laptop shut, then winced. Mom hated it when she did that. Apologizing with a pat, she walked casually into the kitchen.

Mom was chopping onions. "Fresh pea-and-onion soup for dinner, Mads."

"Yum," said Maddy. She would actually prefer pizza. But Maddy thought this was a time to be extra agreeable. "Mom, can I ask you something?"

"Sure." Mom poured some olive oil into a pot.

"Okay, so, um," started Maddy. "I think we should start raising bees." Maddy closed her eyes, then opened one, peeking for Mom's reaction.

Mom scraped the chopped onions off the cutting board into the pot. "Huh. Bees. Okay, give me your pitch."

"Pitch?" said Maddy.

"Yes, Ms. CEO," said Mom. "A pitch is a summary of your project. It should be short but strong enough to convince your audience. Me, in this case."

Maddy liked it when her mom called her a CEO. She dove in, making up a pitch as she went. She tried to end strong.

"This is my chance to do my part. I want to bring back the bees. And make sure all the crops in California, and other places too, will be fertilized each year."

Mom listened carefully. "I like that you want to do your part. But I'm not sure about hives in our backyard."

Maddy tried not to scowl. "Why?"

"Mads, so many reasons," said Mom. "One, it's a lot of work. Two, we don't have enough room out there. Three, we might want to get a dog one day."

Maddy's eyes widened at that part. "And he wouldn't be able to run around freely if we had bees."

Mom's reasons made sense. And the one about a dog was pretty darn convincing!

"Well, where could I keep bees?" asked Maddy. She shifted away from dogs to the subject at hand. "The park?"

"I doubt that's allowed," said Mom.

"How about that empty lot by Darcy's house?" said Maddy.

"No, that's private property, sweetie," said Mom. "You need a spot with lots of space. A spot that's close to home. And that you visit regularly so you can care for them."

Maddy gasped. Of course! There was only one place she spent as much time as at home.

"School!" she said.

"School?" said Mom. "But I'm pretty sure bees need to be isolated. Just so there's no danger of anyone getting stung. You'd need them to be separate, but open to the air."

"We have it!" yelled Maddy, jumping up and down. "The atrium. That place between the auditorium and the office, with the glass wall! It's perfect!"

Chapter Three

"Come on!" Maddy grabbed Darcy's hand, darting through the school gate.

"Bye Mom," she called, turning to wave. They'd arrived at school early. Maddy needed to talk to Mr. Michael, the garden teacher.

As they hurried to the school garden, Maddy silently practiced her pitch. A foursquare ball came flying toward them. Darcy caught it.

Amina raced around the corner of the garden shed. She was their friend who had moved from Syria last year. Seeing them, she ran even faster and stopped. She panted and giggled.

"I should have known it was you," said Darcy with a laugh. She tossed the ball to Amina.

Ever since Maddy had taught Amina foursquare, Amina played it every day. It was her favorite thing about America, she joked.

"Where are you going?" Amina tucked the ball under her arm.

"To start a new project," said Maddy. She continued on around the garden shed. "A super important one. We're going to save the earth!"

Darcy rolled her eyes and giggled. "She's exaggerating slightly. But it IS a cool project. Come with us, Amina!"

Amina tossed the ball over to the foursquare court. She skipped along with them.

Mr. Michael sat on a stump in the school garden. He drank coffee from a glass jar. Spread out around him were cardboard seedling cups and packets of seeds.

"Yo, girls," said Mr. Michael, looking up from his clipboard. He had a smile on his face. A droplet of coffee dripped off his beard. Maddy tried not to giggle.

"Yo!" said Amina. She loved American slang.

"Morning!" said Darcy.

"Hi," said Maddy. Her heart ran fast. What if he said no? She took a breath. "You know how you like having things at school that teach us to be good to the environment?"

"Yep, totally," said Mr. Michael. "Good stewards of the earth. That's my job. Why, you have something in mind?"

Darcy urged Maddy on with her eyes. Amina listened with interest. Maddy squared her shoulders.

"I think we should have a beehive," she said. "I read that bees are disappearing. And that cities are actually really good places to have hives."

She pulled a paper from her pocket and unfolded it. "I looked up this list of other schools that have beehives. So I know it's allowed. And I would start a Bee Team to take care of them. You wouldn't have to do anything."

She stopped, out of breath from talking so fast. She looked at Mr. Michael.

"Keeping bees is a stellar idea," he began. Maddy gave a little clap. "But," he continued, "we don't have the money to buy them."

He held out the clipboard to her. "We're over budget for the year. We've put up solar panels, installed a water bottle filler, and built a bat house. We can't afford another big project."

Maddy bit her lip. "What if . . ." she began. "I got the bees for free?"

"Yeah, free works," said Mr. Michael. "But how?"

Maddy hadn't gotten that far yet. But as she opened her mouth to say so, Amina broke in.

"I know where!" Amina said. "My parents met a beekeeper a while ago. Honey is special in Syria. When we moved here, my parents looked for the best honey around.

"And they found it! Right here in the city. I'll bring you, after school."

Chapter
Four

Amina told them all about the beekeeper. "She taught me a lot about bees. When a colony gets too big, it needs to be divided. Perhaps she'd donate some to our school!"

Just then, the bell rang. The sound of one thousand feet racing on the blacktop thundered in the air.

"Okay, gang, great job," yelled Mr. Michael over the noise. He stood up and stretched. "You better get to morning circle. Let me know how it goes with the beekeeper today!"

The girls ran off, backpacks thumping. Maddy rounded the corner of the garden shed. Her shoulder brushed against the butterfly bush, purple with blooms.

Bees loved the butterfly bush. She had seen them buzzing around it before. This was a perfect home for a new hive!

After school, Maddy and Darcy met on the sidewalk. Maddy's parents or

Darcy's grandma waited for them most days.

Dad was there today, chatting with Amina's mom. Amina and her family used to live on Maddy's block. They had just moved to an apartment a few minutes away.

"Mama!" shouted Amina, bursting out of the school gate. "We've got to bring Maddy and Darcy to the community garden. They need to meet Diana the beekeeper."

"Oh," said Dad. "Is this part of the plan? Did Mr. Michael say yes?"

Maddy explained everything. "If we can get the bees and the hive for free, we can have them!"

"Today is pretty busy," said Amina's mom. "I have some shopping to do."

"I can bring them." Maddy's dad shrugged. "I love that garden, although it makes me jealous. The slugs eat everything we grow in our backyard."

Dad and Amina's mom started talking about gardening. Maddy sighed and grabbed her friends' arms.

"Come on, you guys," she said, "let's start. If we don't, they'll talk forever."

Dad caught up by the time the girls reached the corner. "Amina, I told your mom I'd bring you home around 5 p.m. Sound okay?" he asked.

They reached the community garden in about ten minutes. It was in a quiet area and surrounded by trees. Locals liked to walk their dogs in the big empty lot nearby.

Maddy stopped to throw a tennis ball to a Labrador retriever. Then she pushed open the creaky garden gate.

Wooden planter boxes filled the area. Wood chips covered the ground.

Maddy smelled dirt, compost, and jasmine. A hummingbird dipped into a red flower on a bush. A squirrel darted along the fence.

Darcy, Amina, and Dad pushed in behind Maddy. They all looked around.

"Hmm," said Amina. "Let me try to remember where the bee lady is."

A movement off to the left caught Maddy's eye. She pointed. "There!" she said.

She took a step, looking closer at the person digging in a planter box. Then she stopped in surprise.

Ravi? He lived on her block. He had come to her Pet Camp. That was her very first business from last summer.

"Hi Ravi," she said. "Do you have a garden here?"

"Oh, hi, Maddy," he said, looking up. "Yeah, my grandpa brings me here every Tuesday. He's over there, looking for a trowel." Ravi pointed to a shed.

"Oh," said Maddy. "Well, um, do you know where the beekeeper is?"

"Yeah, I know," said Ravi, jumping up. He brushed his hands on his shorts. He ran toward the back of the garden.

"You guys!" Maddy called.

Amina was wandering in the opposite direction. Dad and Darcy were examining something in one of the boxes. They all looked up.

"Come on! Ravi knows where the bee lady is!"

Ravi was already near the back of the garden. The land began to slope upwards as it approached the fence.

Maddy walked toward him. She saw boxes filled with dark, rich earth and new baby plants. Other boxes had the brittle remains of last year's crops.

Ravi was waiting by the back fence. Right on the other side, someone stood looking at a cluster of white wooden boxes. Beehives, Maddy knew.

Bees buzzed in and out of the boxes. The person wore a white suit and helmet. He or she looked, Maddy thought, like an astronaut.

"This is the bee lady!" said Ravi.

Amina ran up. "Her name is Diana, not 'the bee lady.' "

The person removed her helmet, revealing a friendly face. "That's okay. I go by 'bee lady' all the time!"

Then she looked at Amina. "Oh, lovely to see you again, Amina. What can I do for you? Did you come here to buy some honey? I have plenty over there in the shed."

Maddy looked sideways at her dad. He just raised his eyebrows at her. She was the CEO, his look suggested. She turned back to Diana.

"Maybe," said Maddy, stepping forward hesitantly. "But actually, we came to talk to you. We were hoping you could, well, give us some bees."

Maddy talked faster. "Only if you have enough, of course. Our school wants to start a hive. But we don't have the money to buy one. And Amina thought maybe your hive was big enough to divide up."

Diana tilted her head. She made a sad face that told Maddy the news was not good.

Did Diana understand that Maddy was doing this for the greater good? To help the environment? Maddy's cheeks burned.

Darcy jumped in. "We know that we need more bees in cities. Because of monoculture! And Maddy wants to save the farms, and the avocados."

"Because of guacamole!" Amina added helpfully.

"I love guacamole!" chimed in Ravi.

Diana shook her head. "I'm so sorry, kiddos. I can tell you want to help. And I wish I could be of service. My hive has been growing, yes.

"But I'm having trouble supporting myself. I can't afford to give any bees away. I'm a good beekeeper, but I'm a terrible business person!"

Amina grabbed Maddy's shoulder. Darcy grinned at her. Dad nudged Maddy.

Ravi threw his arms up. "Maddy's the best business person! She did a fun pet camp. Even if she forget to tell me to bring a real cat and not a pretend one. She also did a pop-up movie theater. She saved the block party.

"And she did something at Christmas. I think wrapping presents, but I'm not sure. We were at basketball camp that day. But basically, she's like a real live business CEO. Maybe she can raise the money for you!"

"She can!" said Darcy.

"And we'll help!" said Amina.

"Go for it, Mads," said Dad.

"Ravi!" called someone. "Time to go home. Garden's closing!"

Chapter Five

A Sweet Plan

Maddy promised she'd come up with a way to raise the money to save Diana's business. She said goodbye.

"You have my phone number," called Diana. "Let me know what you come up with!"

All the way home, the girls and Ravi talked about the new challenge. Dad walked behind them with Ravi's grandpa.

"I feel like I'm getting more and more behind," said Maddy. They walked along the busy street, past shops and cafés, and people getting off the streetcar after a day's work.

"First I wanted to save the bees. Now we have to first save Diana's business. And then the bees."

"Yeah, but Diana was cool and nice," said Darcy. "I'm glad we're helping her!"

"What will we do?" asked Amina.

They passed the bakery. The smell made Maddy's stomach rumble. The line out the door made her brain ping.

Really, was there anything people liked more than cookies? "Bake sale!"

"Ooh, we can sell cookies made with honey!" said Darcy.

"Diana's honey!" said Amina, her eyes wide with excitement. "We have

some jars of it. I'm sure my mother won't mind if we use some."

"Perfect!" said Maddy, clapping. She'd been baking with Mom as long as Maddy could remember.

A bake sale would be a breeze. She'd done one before for school. They were raising money for a new playground.

"Should we sell the treats in the park? Like the school bake sale?" Maddy asked.

"I have a better idea." Ravi squeezed between Maddy and Darcy. "The farmers market. Everyone's in a good mood there. And people in a good mood always buy stuff."

Maddy nodded. She thought of the people lining up to pay five dollars for strawberries.

Her parents were always extra generous at the farmers market. Her mom said she liked to support local merchants.

"That's a good idea." Then she sighed. "But we still have to figure out how to pay for the ingredients. This is always the hardest part!"

This was a problem Maddy had tackled with her other businesses. It wasn't exactly new to her. This time, she wasn't sure how to tackle it.

"You guys," said Darcy, looking up. "I think it's starting to rain!"

Maddy felt a rush of happiness. In California, where drought was common, rain was always welcome. But she didn't want to get soaked!

She pulled her sweatshirt up. They hurried on, but the drops came faster. They reached the corner of Twelfth Avenue.

Maddy stopped in front of the Pie Place. Its glass windows were steaming. Maddy looked back at her dad.

The Pie Place had been the site of several moments of inspiration for Maddy's previous businesses. She thought maybe it was time to make another visit.

"Dad?" she called back. "Can we go to the Pie Place?"

Everyone pushed inside, laughing and shaking off wet hair. Ravi pulled off his dripping sweatshirt.

Maddy noticed his shirt underneath. He wore a yellow sports jersey. *Pam's Pizza* was written across the back.

"What does your shirt mean?" she asked Ravi. They filed up to the counter.

"What?" he asked. "Oh yeah. Pam's Pizza sponsored us."

"Sponsored?" asked Amina. She always wanted to learn new English words. Maddy was glad she'd asked. She didn't know what it meant, either.

"It means that they gave us the money for the uniforms. Then they get their name on it. And they get free advertising."

"So it's a win-win?" said Maddy.

But Ravi was peering in the glass case at the pies on display. Maddy thought while everyone ordered.

Ravi got a slice of chicken pot pie. Darcy and Amina asked for the strawberry rhubarb. Dad got carrot soup. Ravi's grandpa had hot tea.

They carried their goodies over to the wooden table. It was Maddy's turn. But there was something besides pie on her mind.

"Hello, my dear," said Aliza. Aliza and Rasheed owned the Pie Place. They had always been big supporters of Maddy's businesses. Now Maddy hoped they would support her in another way.

"Aliza?" she began. "Can I make a business proposition?"

"A business proposition?" said Aliza, opening her eyes wide. "That sounds interesting. Here, let's take a seat." She ushered Maddy to a table with stools.

Peeking over her shoulder, Maddy gave her friends a quick look. Then she turned back to Aliza and pulled herself onto a stool.

"And you can't have a meeting without a treat," said Aliza. She placed a raspberry tart in front of each of them. "I always think better with sugar."

Maddy giggled, glad her mom wasn't there. Mom would say she needed some protein or vegetable soup. Maddy took a bite of tart instead.

"Okay, what's up?" said Aliza.

Maddy felt a little shy. She felt like she was trying too hard to be a grown-up. But on the other hand, Aliza was treating her like one!

She sat up a little straighter and cleared her throat. Her pitch was getting more complicated.

"We want to sell treats at the farmers market to raise money. To help the bee lady at the community garden.

"So she can get enough money to give us bees. For our school. So we can save the crops. And the farms. And all food, basically."

Aliza nodded. "I know about the bee crisis. This is a wonderful plan! We use many fruits here that are pollinated by bees. But how can I help?"

"Well," began Maddy. She looked at Ravi, who was blowing on his hot chicken pot pie. "Ravi's shirt gave me the idea. Would you maybe be willing to sponsor us?

"If you gave us money for the ingredients, we could put your name somewhere. Like on the sign at our stand at the farmers market. You'd get free advertising."

"Win-win!" shouted Ravi.

Aliza laughed. "Yes, we'd be happy to do that. In fact, we can eliminate a step. We can supply the ingredients. We buy flour, sugar, eggs, and so on in bulk. We can afford to spare some. Especially for such a good cause."

"Yes!" cheered Maddy. "Thank you, Aliza!"

"But there's another issue." Aliza paused to take a bite of her tart. "To sell edible goods legally, you must bake them in a kitchen that conforms to city health codes. Does yours?"

"Um, what?" Maddy asked, mid-chew. This was not an issue she had encountered before.

"Yes, I know it sounds crazy," said Aliza. "But it's the law. You must bake the food in a professional restaurant-quality kitchen."

Maddy thought of her big and comfy kitchen at home. It was basically her favorite room in the world. But it was hardly restaurant-quality.

The old ceramic sink was chipped. The counter was stained and banged up. The oven's handle had just broken off last week. They had to use tongs and a pot holder to open it.

Homework in process was generally spread out over the island. Mom's teapot was always somewhere in the way. Homey, yes. Professional, no. Maddy's heart sunk.

At that moment, the kitchen door opened. Rasheed pushed through, carrying a tray. It was lined with paper and tartlets studded with blueberries.

The door was one of those restaurant kinds that swing both ways. It swung

a few times before settling. But Maddy glimpsed the sparkling kitchen on the other side.

So that's what a professional kitchen looks like, she thought. She dragged

her eyes back to Aliza's. "No," Maddy said. "Our kitchen is, well, just regular."

Aliza's head was tilted slightly. When she met Maddy's gaze, she smiled. "Ours isn't. And after 7 p.m. every night, it's empty, too."

It was official. The Pie Place was their sponsor. And they'd provide both the ingredients and the kitchen.

Aliza and Rasheed gave Maddy, Darcy, Amina, and Ravi a handshake. The kids filed out the door.

"We'll see you Friday!" called Maddy, waving.

The rain had stopped, and the late-afternoon sun had broken through.

Raindrops sparkled on the sidewalk, car windows, and parking meters.

The group turned left off the commercial street. They walked along a quieter block of houses and apartments. They passed under a tree and raindrops fell on them.

"Yikes!" Ravi bolted ahead.

Maddy laughed and gave a little skip. "Okay, guys," she said. "What should we bake? Remember, it has to have honey."

"I'd like to make my grandmother's honey cake," said Amina.

"Once my mom made these sugar cookies with honey instead of sugar. And with this amazing sugar glazey stuff on top. I almost died. They were so delicious," said Darcy.

"I don't know any recipes." Ravi frowned and kicked a pebble. "But wait. Can it be a drink? Because I had some honey lemonade once. It was so good! Can I make that?"

"Yeah, sure," said Darcy. "They'll need something to wash our treats down with. Maddy, what are you making?"

They passed the Wolf house. Amina had lived there when she'd arrived in the city last year. Maddy's house was just a few houses past it.

"I don't know." Maddy trailed her hand along a lavender bush. She squeezed a flower and smelled her fingers. *Mmm.* Lavender went great with honey.

A bee landed on the flower next to her. She smiled. Bees loved lavender.

They arrived at Maddy's house. Dad went in and came back with his keys. He had to drive Amina home.

"Bye, Amina." Maddy waved to her other friends. Ravi lived a few houses away. Darcy was around the corner.

"See you Friday. Bring your recipes. Don't forget the honey, Amina!"

Maddy ran into the kitchen. She grabbed her mom's cookie cookbook off the shelf, and turned to the index. "H . . . ha . . . hi . . . ho . . . honey!"

She grabbed a teacup. "Can we have tea, Mom? I need to do a cookie test!"

The rest of the week flew by in a flurry of cookie crumbs. Finally it was Friday night.

Ding dong! Maddy threw open the front door. Darcy and Ravi stood there, bouncing excitedly in the fading light.

"Bye, Mom!" Maddy slammed the door. "Come on, guys! We have so much to bake!"

They sprinted down the block and around the corner. Just as they arrived at the café, a car door slammed. Amina joined them, waving goodbye to her dad.

"Perfect timing," she said, putting one arm through Maddy's. In the other, she clutched a large jar of honey.

The café looked bright and cozy. Maddy pushed open the glass doors and the bell jingled. Rasheed looked up from the counter and threw his arms in the air.

"Our bakers have arrived!" he shouted. "We've been waiting for you!"

Darcy and Amina giggled. Ravi laughed and jumped up and down. Maddy felt warm, like she'd just had a cup of hot honey lemonade.

The kids followed Rasheed into the café's kitchen. Aliza waited for them just inside.

Maddy looked around. She counted four baking stations set up in different locations. Each had a set of metal mixing bowls, spoons and spatulas, and baking sheets.

"Your stations await," said Aliza. "Now, tell me what you're baking today. And I'll gather your ingredients."

They pulled out their recipes. Amina had a handwritten sheet with her grandmother's Syrian honey cake recipe.

Ravi explained that he was making honey lemonade. Darcy had printed out her honey-lemon cookie recipe. And then Aliza turned to Maddy. "And you, Maddy?" she asked.

Maddy took a cookbook out of her bag. "I'm making honey-lavender madeleines. They're my favorite cookies to dip in tea. I taste-tested them the other day."

"Oh my," said Aliza. "That sounds divine. All right, my dears, to your stations. Let the baking, and lemonade making, begin!"

Chapter Eight

At the Farmers Market

HONEY

Maddy couldn't believe it was actually the big day.

"Move it to the right a bit." Amina's hands were on her hips. She looked at their hand-painted banner.

"Okay," said Darcy. She moved the sign to the right and re-stuck the tape. "Like this?"

Maddy finished arranging the goods on the table. She looked around them.

To their left was the Lopez Farm. A woman was chatting with the owner. She wanted more of the butter lettuce she'd tried the week before.

On their right was an almond grower. He was handing out samples of maple-cinnamon roasted almonds. Thinking of samples, Maddy looked for the avocado seller.

Ravi came staggering down the aisle of produce, food, and flower booths. He pulled a little red wagon. Inside were paper cups and two large jugs of lemonade.

"Phew." Maddy scooted out inside of the table to unload. "I was getting worried about you!"

"Sorry," said Ravi. "I had to walk slowly so the jugs wouldn't tip. Where should we put them?"

Maddy surveyed the table. "Hmm. Let's move the cookies here. And put the lemonade on the end. Maybe you should pour some cups."

Ravi started pouring. Maddy joined Amina to look at the sign.

Bring back the bees!! it proclaimed in giant rainbow letters. *Buy a sweet treat to support our local beekeeper! Sponsored by The Pie Place.* She had added some bees buzzing around flowers.

She'd stuck in butterflies and hummingbirds, too. They didn't make honey, but they did pollinate flowers. She figured it was okay.

It was a beautiful sign. Maddy hoped it would encourage people to buy their goods.

A woman walked up to the stand. She carried a shopping basket with carrots sticking out. Darcy pointed.

Maddy slipped behind the table, her heart racing. Their first sale!

"I'll take two cakes and a lemonade."

The woman held out ten dollars.

Bring Back the Bees!!

Buy a sweet treat to support our local Beekeeper!

Sponsored by The Pie Place!

As Maddy made the change, the woman looked at the sign. "So how will buying baked goods save the bees?"

It was a good question. If only the answer weren't so long.

"Well, I want to have bees at school," Maddy said. "But we don't have enough money. So I went to a beekeeper.

"But she said her business wasn't doing well. She couldn't afford to give us any bees. So we decided to have a bake sale to raise money for her."

The woman paused for a moment, thinking. Then she gave a little head shake and smiled. "Well, good luck, kids!"

The woman packed her cake in her basket. A line had formed behind her. Ravi had been right. People at a farmers market were in a good mood!

Live bluegrass music floated from the corner. The smell of homemade tamales wafted from the other end. Parents pushed strollers. Friends stopped to chat.

It felt like a fair. And just like at a fair, people were more than happy to spend money on homemade goodies!

Maddy and her friends were busy working their booth. But something bothered her.

What had she told the first lady? That the beekeeper's business wasn't doing well. Would selling cookies truly improve her business?

They'd give her a one-time gift. But when that money was gone, then what? Would they keep having bake sales?

Maddy knew that wasn't possible. She and her friends had other things to do. They couldn't man a farmers market booth every weekend.

A bake sale had sounded fun. And it was fun. But did a complicated problem need a more complicated solution?

Suddenly Maddy did not feel like a CEO. She felt like a little kid. A little kid who thought that you could save the world by selling cookies and lemonade.

A voice broke into her thoughts. "These cookies are wonderful! What kind of honey did you use?"

Maddy looked up. An older man stood munching on one of Darcy's frosted sugar cookies. "Um, the honey's from the beekeeper at the community garden."

"Oh, do you have some here?"

Maddy started to shake her head, but Amina interrupted her. "Yes!" She grabbed her tote bag from under the table. "It's still in my bag from the baking the other night."

She pulled out the honey and showed it to the man.

Maddy froze. She turned her head and glanced at the almond seller. He was still handing out samples.

She looked at the Lopez Farm stand. She thought of the woman asking for more of the lettuce she loved.

Selling cookies made with Diana's honey was a great step. But wouldn't selling the honey itself be even better? And help make people fall in love with it too?

She turned around, looking for Mom. She was talking with the cheese seller across the way. "Mom!" Maddy said. "I need Popsicle sticks!"

Chapter nine

"I know I have them in my craft stuff." Maddy and Mom ran-walked the four blocks to their house. As they hurried along, Maddy explained her plan.

"If people taste the honey and love it, they'll want to buy it. And hopefully keep buying it. We won't be helping Diana once. We'll start a whole thing."

"That's brilliant, Mads," Mom said. She gave her a half-hug.

"You're helping her create a sustainable, long-term business. Do you want to call Diana to make sure she has enough honey?"

At home, Maddy tucked the Popsicle sticks in her backpack. Mom gave Maddy her phone as they headed to the market.

"That's wonderful!" said Diana, over the phone. "You're not only raising money for me. You're going to set up a customer base!"

Diana took inventory, counting the jars of honey. "I'm here every day until about 5 p.m. So come on by to get them whenever you like."

"Okay!" said Maddy. She and Mom entered the bustle of the market.

Maddy knew there was more to figure out. But it was hard to talk over the noise of the crowd. She said bye and gave Mom her phone back.

Mom stopped to buy flowers. Maddy continued on, her mind whirring.

"Yay, you're back!" said Darcy.

"Here's the honey," said Amina. She held out the jar with the pretty hand-drawn label.

Maddy dipped a Popsicle stick into the jar. A teardrop-shaped dollop of honey, amber-colored, lay glistening on the tip. It was beautiful.

The kids gazed at it for a moment. And then Ravi stuck it in his mouth. "Yum!" he said.

"Ravi!" said Maddy.

"I had to be sure our product was good!"

Maddy laughed. He had a point. She dipped three more sticks and passed them out.

"This is going to be easy to sell," said Darcy. "It's so good!"

A mom and two little kids strolled up. They looked at the cookies.

Darcy nudged Maddy and she stepped forward. "Um, these cookies and cakes are made with local honey. Would you like a taste?"

"I would!" said the boy. "I love honey." Amina dipped a stick and passed it over. "Mmmm," said the boy.

Amina made samples for the mom and sister, too. "How much is a jar?" asked the mom, looking at the label.

Maddy thought quickly. "Ten dollars."

The mom paused. Maddy knew ten dollars was a lot. But this was not your average honey. Just like the strawberries people lined up for were not your average strawberries. They were worth paying more for.

Still. Maybe an incentive would help?

"And for your first jar, we'll deliver to your house. Free!" she added. "Tonight!"

The mom laughed. "That's a pretty good perk. I'll take two jars." She handed over a twenty-dollar bill.

Maddy would need the woman's address. She grabbed her little notebook with the tiny pencil attached. She kept them in her pocket.

Maddy felt a little silly. She should have brought a clipboard. But this would do in a pinch. *Rolling with the punches*, she remembered.

She took down the address and phone number. Then she noted, *2 jars*. As the morning wore on, the names and addresses grew.

The kids worked hard. Ravi called out "Honey samples!" Amina scooped. Darcy sold the goods. Maddy took the money and wrote addresses.

There was no time to chat. But inside, Maddy's mind was racing.

How on earth was she going to deliver all these jars? She could get over to the community garden after the market. But then what?

Even with her friends, and Mom and Dad, this would take hours and hours. Why had she promised delivery tonight? And not tomorrow? Or even over the next week?

Maddy grabbed Darcy's arm.

"Darcy, we have to stop selling," she said. "I think I made a huge mistake. There's no way we can deliver all these jars today."

Darcy opened her mouth to reply. But a girl arrived at the table, out of breath. "My dad sent me to buy five jars! We want them delivered to five different people!"

Maddy's heart sunk. She turned back to Darcy, but she wasn't there.

"Where can I write the addresses?" asked the girl. Maddy sighed and turned back. This honey mess was getting stickier and stickier.

Chapter
Ten

It took a while to write down all five addresses. The girl ran off.

Maddy blew out a big puff of air. Then Drew skidded in front of her. He was with his best friend, Will.

"Can we have some samples?" Drew asked. "Everyone's talking about it."

"Yeah, and my mom wants me to buy a jar," said Will. "She likes honey in her tea."

"I'm not going to sell anymore," said Maddy. "But you can have samples."

Where was Amina? She had the Popsicle sticks. Maddy turned. Her friends were at the back of the booth. What were they whispering about?

Darcy ran over. "Don't worry about anything," she told Maddy.

"What?" asked Maddy.

Amina joined them. "Here," she said, scooping samples for Drew and Will.

"And we're definitely not going to stop selling," said Darcy firmly. She passed the notebook to Will. "Here, write down your address. And that will be ten dollars, please."

"But Darcy! We have to stop!"

"Nope." Darcy crossed her arms. "We have it figured out. No questions. Just keep taking orders. And meet us at the community garden at four o'clock."

Somehow, letting someone else tell her what to do, giving up control, just once, felt wonderful. Maddy shrugged. And she kept on taking orders.

At one o'clock, the kids cleaned up and said goodbye. "See you at four!" said Darcy as she ran off.

Her parents were picking her up on the corner. They were giving Amina and Ravi a ride home, too. Mom and Maddy walked home.

That afternoon, Maddy and Dad went to the garden early. They wanted to talk to Diana.

They found the beekeeper in her shed. She was looking over jars glistening in the late-afternoon sun.

"Hi!" said Maddy, walking up shyly.

"Well, hello!" Diana turned around.

"You have lots of honey." Maddy marveled at the wall of jars.

"Yes. It's getting the customers that's been the problem. Until now, that is!"

They spent the next hour organizing jars. Referring to her notebook, Maddy put jars in paper bags. She wrote on the addressees with a marker.

It was fun being so busy and professional. Maddy let her worries fade into the background.

"That's the last one," she said. She stepped back to look over their work.

Dozens of bags sat around the community garden. Surveying her work gave Maddy a warm feeling inside. Until she remembered that now she had to deliver them.

Was it four o'clock yet? As she looked at her watch, she heard a voice. Another voice. A bunch of voices!

The gate creaked. Maddy saw a line of people entering the garden.

The first was Darcy. Then her grandma, Poh-Poh, followed, pulling a metal cart. Poh-Poh used it for grocery shopping. But now it was empty.

"I'm ready to work!" said Poh-Poh to Maddy. She smiled and pointed to her cart. "Give me the honey!"

Ravi was there with his little red wagon. Amina and her parents. All their neighbors. Kids rode scooters. Parents pushed strollers. Drew and Will had wired crates to their bikes.

Everyone was chatting and laughing. They spread out around the planter.

Maddy stood frozen with her notebook in hand. What was going on?

Last of all filed in Rasheed, Aliza, and Mr. Michael. "Yo!" said Mr. Michael.

Rasheed waved at Maddy.

"I guess it was a success," Aliza called.

"Um, yeah," said Maddy. "But I don't know what's happening now."

Darcy ran up to Maddy. "I'll tell you!" Amina and Ravi joined them. "You do everything for other people. You saved the block party."

"And you raised money for my grandparents to come to America," said Amina.

"And you had an awesome pet camp," added Ravi. "I hope you have one every summer for ever and ever!"

"We thought it was everyone else's turn to help you," said Darcy. "We asked the block after the market. And everyone wanted to help. With this many people, we can get the honey delivered super fast."

Mr. Michael nodded. "Dude, the power of community. Pretty awesome."

"Thank you," Maddy said. She hugged Darcy and Amina hugged them both. Ravi stepped away.

"No hugs for me! Time to work!" And he picked up an armful of bags.

One hour later, Maddy collapsed on a bench under an apple tree. The last bag of honey was delivered.

The neighbors and friends had gone home. Only Maddy, her parents, Drew, and Diana remained.

Diana opened the garden shed. "I think it's time for a break." She took out a jar.

She sliced a loaf of bread. She spread gooey honey on the slices.

"Oh, I just remembered!" said Mom. She reached into her tote bag for a thermos. "I have tea!" Mom poured the tea into paper cups.

"Cheers," she said. Everyone clinked before taking a bite.

Drew stuffed his bread into his mouth whole. He looked over the fence at Diana's white boxes.

"These hives are pretty cool," he said. "I think I'll do something on bees for my science project."

"I can answer any questions you have," said Diana. "I owe your sister! If even a quarter of these buyers become regular customers, I'll be able to relax, financially.

"Maddy, I should be able to give your school a nice-sized bee colony to start with. Maybe next week?"

Maddy licked her sticky finger and sat up straight. She had been so focused on the honey sale. She'd almost forgotten the whole reason she was selling it.

"That's so great! Thank you!"

"Way to save the earth, Mads," said Dad. He clapped her on the back. Mom squeezed her shoulder. Maddy smiled and leaned against the bench.

A bee buzzed by. A hummingbird zoomed. She took another bite and closed her eyes. *Yum, avocado would be good on this bread, too.*

How was it that the simplest things were the best? Like friends helping friends. Like a community coming together. Like honey on bread.

A GUIDE FOR KID ENTREPRENEURS
Part 4: Writing a Winning Pitch

Entrepreneurs need to convincingly present their business to other people. Their "pitch" asks for permission or financial support. Here are some tips for a great pitch:

- Include why you're qualified to run this business, and your vision for the future (is it one-time or long-term?).

- Memorize the pitch.

- Record yourself and watch the recording. (Did you overuse "um" and "like"?)

- Keep it short—under three minutes.

- Write a second version under five sentences, for occasions when time is limited. This is called an elevator pitch.

EMMA BLAND SMITH
- Author -

Like her character Maddy McGuire, Emma Bland Smith loves coming up with crazy schemes, and writing children's books is her favorite one yet. Her first book was the award-winning Journey: Based on the True Story of OR7, the Most Famous Wolf in the West. Emma also works as a librarian in San Francisco, where she lives with her husband and two kids. (She hopes her neighbors will recognize the setting of the Maddy McGuire series!) Visit emmabsmith.com to learn more about Emma and her other books.

LISSY MARLIN
- Illustrator -

Lissy is an illustrator with a passion and love for animation, visual development, and children's books. She was born and raised in the Dominican Republic before moving to the United States, where she studied illustration at the University of the Arts of Philadelphia. Her passion with illustration and animation truly began after watching Spirited Away. Since then, Hayao Miyazaki has been her biggest artistic influence, while making people smile with beautiful and inspiring images has been her main purpose as an artist. Lissy absolutely loves collecting art books of all kinds, stargazing, traveling, and learning about different languages and cultures.